The Famous Adventure

A Bird-Brained Hen

Jessica Souhami

FRANCES LINCOLN

I'm going to tell you the famous story
of a bird-brained hen called Penny.

And this is how it goes…

One day an acorn fell, BOP!
on Henny Penny's head.

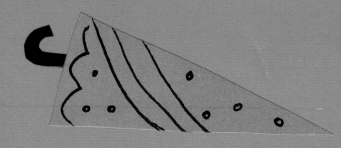

"OOF," she said. "What was that?"

And she looked up.

"The sky must be falling," she said.

"I must go and tell the King."

So Henny Penny hurried along.

And very soon…

"I'm going to tell the King
that the sky is falling," said Penny.
"You can come too."

So Henny Penny and
Ducky Daddles hurried along.

And very soon...

…they met Cocky Locky.
"Hello," said Locky. "Where are
you two going?"

"We're going to tell the King that the sky is falling," said Penny and Daddles. "You can come too."

So Henny Penny, Ducky Daddles
and Cocky Locky hurried along.
And very soon…

…they met Goosey Poosey.
"Hello," said Poosey.
"Where are you three going?"

"We're going to tell the King that the sky is falling," said Penny and Daddles and Locky. "You can come too."

So Henny Penny, Ducky Daddles,
Cocky Locky and Goosey Poosey
hurried along.

And very soon…

…they came to Foxy Loxy's house.

And there was Foxy Loxy at the door.

"Hello!" said Foxy.

"Where are you all going?"

"We're going to tell the King that the sky is falling," said Penny and Daddles and Locky and Poosey. "But *somehow* we've come to your door."

"Quite right!" said Foxy.
"This *is* the quickest way to the
King's Palace. DO COME IN!"
And they were just about to enter
Foxy's house…when…

…Henny Penny peeped inside.
And she saw –

a cooking pot full of boiling water,
a carrot and an onion, neatly chopped,
AND, glinting behind Foxy's back…
the sharp, sharp edge of a big, big
CHOPPER!

"OH NO!" she cried.
"We're for Foxy's SOUP!"
"QUICK BIRDS, FLY!"

And they did!

And back at home, ruffled but safe,
Henny Penny decided not to go to the
King to tell him that the sky was falling.
Well, not today.

And as for Foxy Loxy…
all he had for dinner
was some
very thin
soup.

And that is the end of the story.

First published in Great Britain in 2003 by

Frances Lincoln Limited, 4 Torriano Mews

Torriano Avenue, London NW5 2RZ

w.w.w.franceslincoln.com

British Library Cataloguing in Publication Data available on request

ISBN 0-7112-2025-5

Set in Gill Sans

Printed in Singapore

1 9 8 7 6 5 4 3 2 1